Cosmo
Faces the Forest of Fear

Hi Nolan and Mason!

Never forget what Cosmo would do!
Be GOLDEN and enjoy all of life's treats!

Amulya Veldanda Vadali

Cosmo
Faces the Forest of Fear

By
Amulya Veldanda Vadali

Illustrated by Seriusrin

Dedication

To my parents, Ashok and Lakshmi, who nurtured my love of reading and writing.

To my husband, Shashank, who helped me rediscover my passion.

To my best friend and muse, Cosmo, who will forever have a piece of my heart.

ONCE UPON A TIME, A FAMILY LET A SPECIAL

GOLDEN PUPPY NAMED

COSMO

INTO THEIR HOME AND INTO THEIR HEARTS.

THAT IS WHERE THIS STORY STARTS.

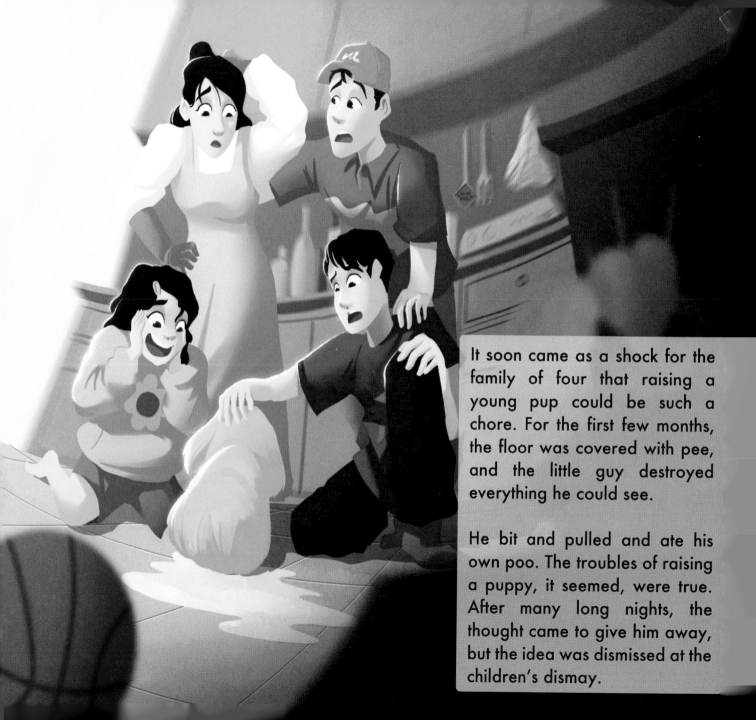

It soon came as a shock for the family of four that raising a young pup could be such a chore. For the first few months, the floor was covered with pee, and the little guy destroyed everything he could see.

He bit and pulled and ate his own poo. The troubles of raising a puppy, it seemed, were true. After many long nights, the thought came to give him away, but the idea was dismissed at the children's dismay.

And within no time, things became good and right. The golden puppy learned to lick instead of bite! From four to five, the family became. They loved him dearly, and he felt the same.

Now, Cosmo was nearing the age of one, and the family was going on vacation for fun. To the grand forest mountains up in the north, with Cosmo's tail wagging, the family set forth.

They hadn't been on vacation for long when Cosmo felt that something was wrong. His wagging tail slowed to a stop. He looked around nervously, and he felt his stomach drop.

The tall hills for the family looked fun and cheery, but the golden pup could sense that something was eerie. For every scent of the forest smelled like fear and the silence of the trees seemed all too queer.

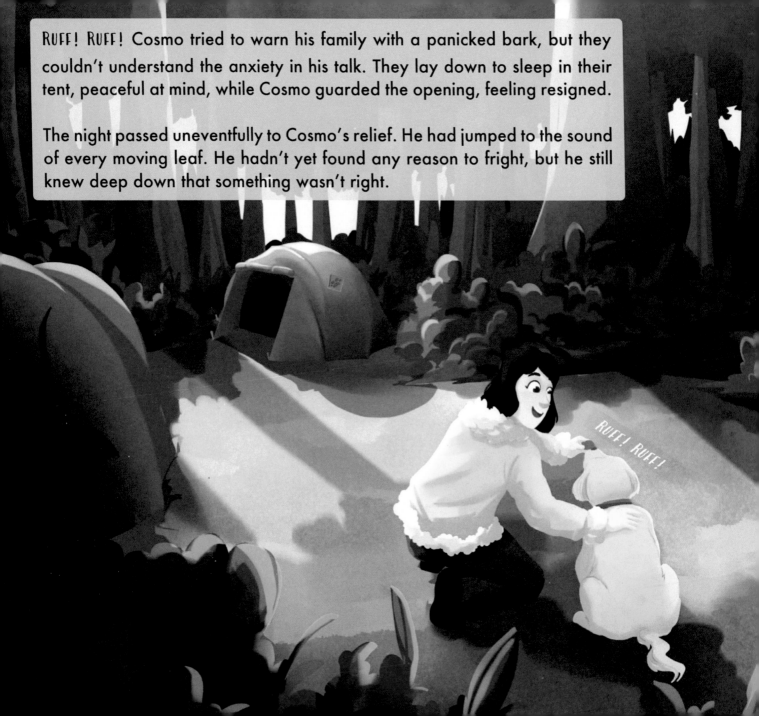

RUFF! RUFF! Cosmo tried to warn his family with a panicked bark, but they couldn't understand the anxiety in his talk. They lay down to sleep in their tent, peaceful at mind, while Cosmo guarded the opening, feeling resigned.

The night passed uneventfully to Cosmo's relief. He had jumped to the sound of every moving leaf. He hadn't yet found any reason to fright, but he still knew deep down that something wasn't right.

The family set out in the morning to hike. Cosmo stayed alert, ready for something to strike. The last place he wanted to go was into the forest of trees, but there was nothing he could do to express his unease.

Everyone seemed carefree and happy except for the golden one. Dad took pictures of Mom, and they watched the kids skip and run. Cosmo ran along at their heels, only stopping for treats. Even in his time of stress, he would not refuse his sweets!

It was after lunch when the family realized a terrible fact. The girl was nowhere to be seen, not even a track. The parents screamed in terror and called for help. Cosmo made his decision and ran off with a yelp.

Cosmo heard his mother shouting his name, but he knew he must find Sis or live in shame. He could sense that a terrible thing lived in the trees and that given a chance, his sister would be seized.

As he ran into the forest, a crow croaked from the canopy of trees as if trying to warn. Cosmo's fear for the forest and love for his sister made him feel torn. But no! His mind was made. He would battle his fright. For his sister, he would do anything—not run, but fight!

Cosmo was going on his way sniffing here and there when out of the bushes flew a creature, giving him a scare. Cosmo barked and got ready to charge, but it was just a skunk—nothing scary or large.

A SKUNK! He turned to flee, but the damage was done. He
stink, and there was nowhere to run. The smell was worse than
lived on his street. He knew to remove the odor would be quite the

Skunk looked at Cosmo with an apology in his eyes, for he had not meant to
but he had been caught by surprise. The golden was quick to forgive, and his tail
began to sway. He loved to make new friends, and he always loved to play!

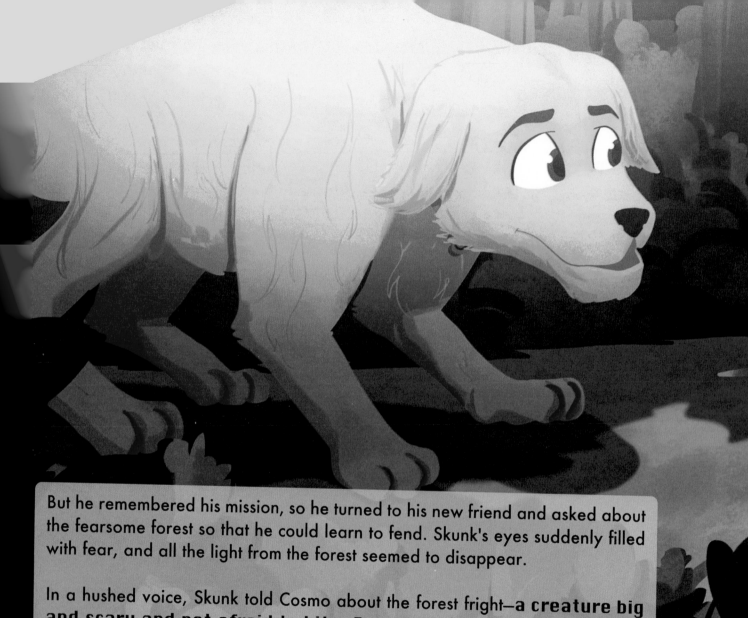

But he remembered his mission, so he turned to his new friend and asked about the fearsome forest so that he could learn to fend. Skunk's eyes suddenly filled with fear, and all the light from the forest seemed to disappear.

In a hushed voice, Skunk told Cosmo about the forest fright—**a creature big and scary and not afraid to bite.** Every animal in the forest feared the terrible beast, wondering and worrying when they would be his next feast.

A feline, Skunk finally revealed, ruled those high up peaks, stalking every creature and pouncing on whom he seeks. **"His eyes,"** Skunk said, **"shine like blazing pits. His pointy teeth and jaws of death could bite anything to bits."**

Having thanked his new friend, Cosmo resumed his journey ahead. Rather than feeling more frightened, he felt surprisingly relieved instead. The monster of the forest, it turned out, was a cat. Cosmo now knew it was just another pesky brat!

However, Cosmo's relief quickly disappeared as he came across a scary sight. Some of the cat's last meal was scattered near a tree, having lost a terrible fight. Cosmo's heart once again pounded against his chest from fear, and from deep within the trees, the beast watched with a leer.

WOOF! WOOF!

A shrill screech suddenly pierced through the chilly air. Cosmo knew he was going deeper and deeper into the big cat's lair. His eyes scanned the woods for a sign of Sis, and he sniffed all around so there was nothing he would miss.

And suddenly, with a cry of relief, the girl ran from the trees! Cosmo let out a bark of joy as his sister gave him a squeeze. He licked the tears from her cheeks, and his tail went wild. She hugged him, scrunched her nose at his stink, and finally smiled.

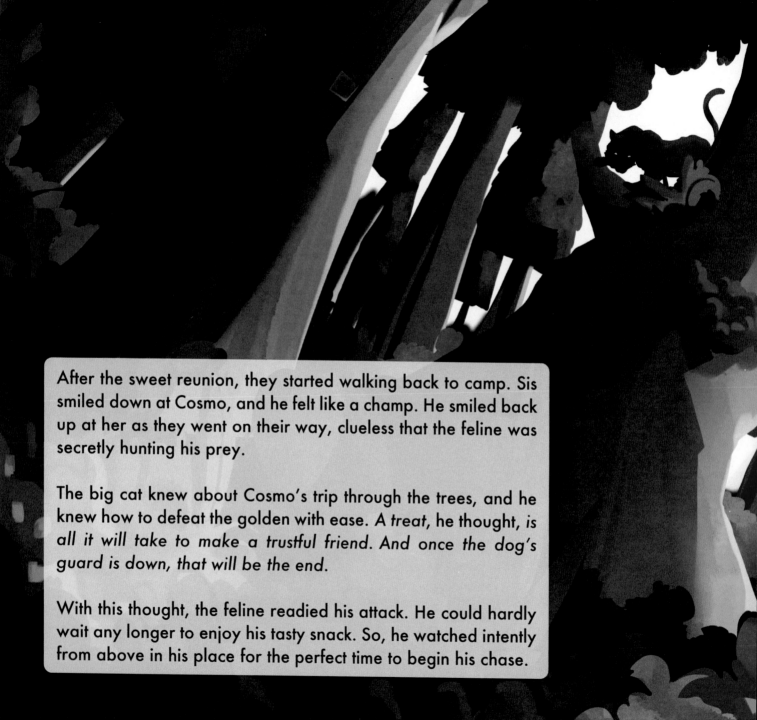

After the sweet reunion, they started walking back to camp. Sis smiled down at Cosmo, and he felt like a champ. He smiled back up at her as they went on their way, clueless that the feline was secretly hunting his prey.

The big cat knew about Cosmo's trip through the trees, and he knew how to defeat the golden with ease. A treat, he thought, *is all it will take to make a trustful friend. And once the dog's guard is down, that will be the end.*

With this thought, the feline readied his attack. He could hardly wait any longer to enjoy his tasty snack. So, he watched intently from above in his place for the perfect time to begin his chase.

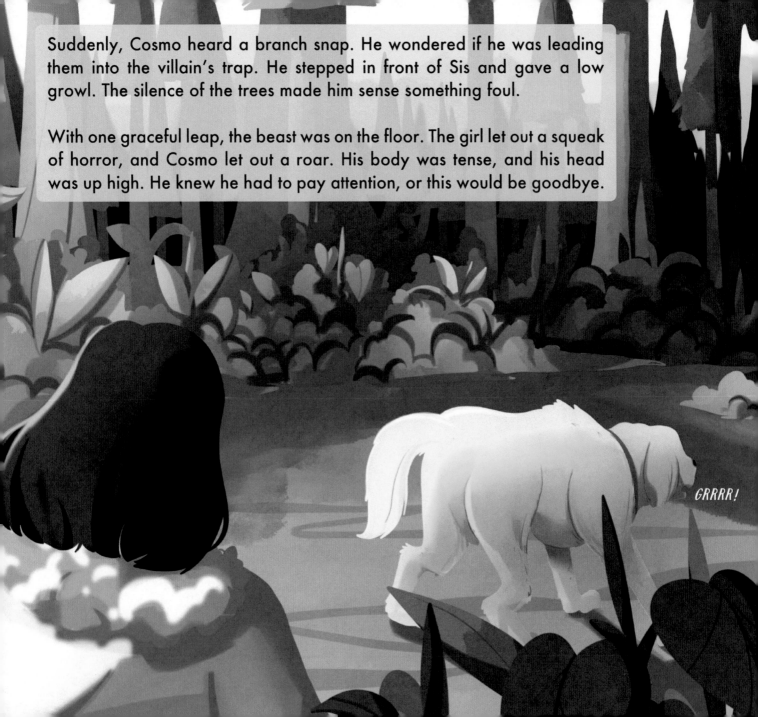

Suddenly, Cosmo heard a branch snap. He wondered if he was leading them into the villain's trap. He stepped in front of Sis and gave a low growl. The silence of the trees made him sense something foul.

With one graceful leap, the beast was on the floor. The girl let out a squeak of horror, and Cosmo let out a roar. His body was tense, and his head was up high. He knew he had to pay attention, or this would be goodbye.

GRRRR!

The big cat stepped forward, a smile on his face. He pushed a treat toward the golden and backed to give some space. Cosmo looked at the snack, his mouth starting to drool. Was *this* a peace offering or a clever way to fool?

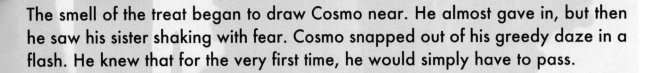

The smell of the treat began to draw Cosmo near. He almost gave in, but then he saw his sister shaking with fear. Cosmo snapped out of his greedy daze in a flash. He knew that for the very first time, he would simply have to pass.

Cosmo shoved the offering away with a swipe of his paw. In the cat's master plan, rejection of the treat was a flaw. The beast's eyes flashed with anger, and his teeth gleamed. Cosmo's mind worked fast for an idea as his sister screamed.

YEET!

The monster leapt, his jaws open and ready to eat the two!
So, Cosmo made a decision and did what he had to do...

THE VILLAIN GOT HIT STRAIGHT IN THE EYES AND LET OUT A CRY!

As the feline shrieked and staggered, his eyes red,
Cosmo courageously charged at him with his head.
He then used his big paws to give the cat a push.
The feline lost his balance and fell on his tush!

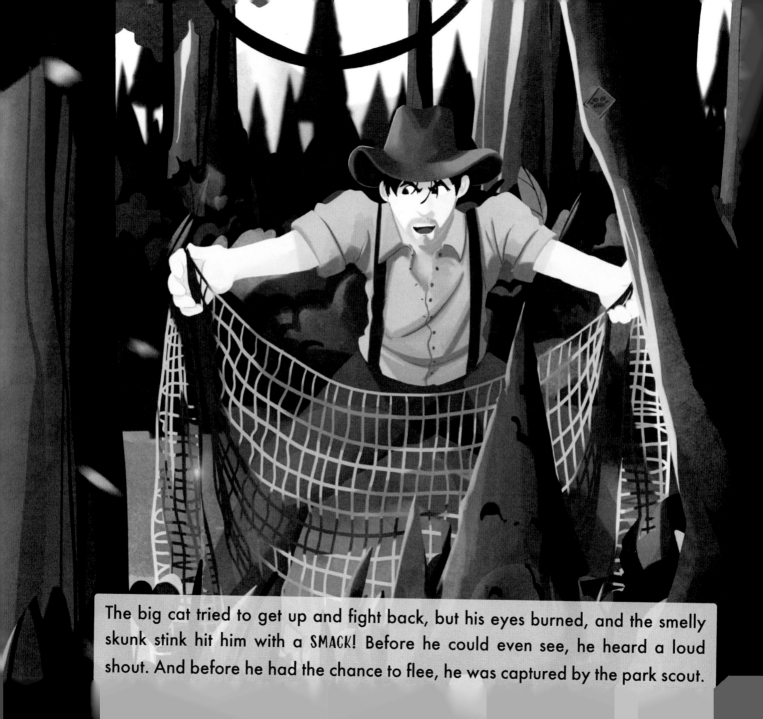

The big cat tried to get up and fight back, but his eyes burned, and the smelly skunk stink hit him with a SMACK! Before he could even see, he heard a loud shout. And before he had the chance to flee, he was captured by the park scout.

Now the feline was hissing at everyone, obviously enraged. Cosmo let out a victory bark when he saw the villain caged. Mom, Dad, and Bro rushed to him and Sis with tears. They hugged and kissed them both and honored Cosmo with...

Cosmo became the hero of the day for Sis and Skunk. He became well known throughout the forest for his wit and spunk. The hills, thereafter, became warm, friendly, and nice. AND THE FELINE ENDED IN THE ZOO, WHERE ALL HE HAS ARE MICE!

THE END

Activity and Questions

Oh no!
Cosmo lost 14 treats
throughout the book!
Can you be his friend and
help him look?

Go back through the book and find one
diamond dog treat in every scene!

Cosmo has some questions for you.
Grab a paper and pencil and answer a few!

1) What is a major theme of the story?

2) What is one of Cosmo's strengths?

3) What is one of Cosmo's weaknesses?

4) What does being brave mean to you?

5) Can you think of a time you were scared to do something, but you were still able to?

6) Draw a picture of that time that you were scared and how you were able to face that fear.

Cosmo had so much fun reading with you!
He'd love to do it again sometime soon!

Made in the USA
Middletown, DE
07 June 2022

66447271R00024